FIREMAN SAM'S STORY TREASURY

Fireman Sam and the Fireworks

story by Diane Wilmer
illustrations by The County Studio

DEAN

It was November 5th, Bonfire Night, and Fireman Sam was planning a big fireworks party for everyone in Pontypandy.

"I'll have two of your biggest boxes of fireworks, please Dilys," he said.

"TWO!" cried Dilys. "That'll cost a lot of money, you know."

"Well, it'll be worth it, Dilys," said Fireman Sam. "I want to put on a good show for the children. I'd rather they came to my bonfire party than stayed at home and messed about with fireworks on their own."

"Quite right, Fireman Sam," said Dilys. "Now, just hold on a minute while I fetch the key to the fireworks cupboard."

While Fireman Sam paid for the fireworks, Dilys's son Norman watched from the back of the shop.

"I wonder if he's picked the box with the brilliant big rocket?" he thought, but he couldn't see very much from where he was standing. He moved a bit closer.

"Ah, Norman, there you are," said his mum. "Come and give Fireman Sam a hand with these boxes, there's a dear."

Norman helped Fireman Sam carry the boxes outside.

"You'll be coming along tonight, won't you Norman?" asked Fireman Sam.

"Of course!" said Norman. "I just wish I could set off all these fireworks myself."

"No, you can't do that," said Fireman Sam. "It's too dangerous, but you can come and watch me set up the fireworks ready for tonight, if you like."

Sarah and James came running out of Bella's cafe.
"Can we watch, too, Uncle Sam?" they asked.
"Yes, you can all come and watch," laughed Fireman Sam. "As long as you promise to do exactly as I say."
"We promise," said the three children.
"Rightio," said Fireman Sam. "I'll see you all later this afternoon, then."

Fireman Sam pedalled slowly up the hill to Pontypandy Fire Station. It was hard work with two big boxes weighing him down, but he finally arrived and climbed off his bike.

He picked up both boxes and set off up the path.

"PHEW!" muttered Fireman Sam. "These are too heavy. I'll have to leave one of them on the path and come back for it in a minute."

He carefully lowered one of the boxes onto the path and carried the other one into the garage. But as soon as Fireman Sam had gone inside, Norman popped out from behind a tree.

"I must see if Fireman Sam's got that big rocket," thought Norman and he lifted the lid off the box of fireworks.

But just as Norman was about to look through the fireworks, he heard the office door slam.

"Bother!" he thought, and hid behind the tree again.

Station Officer Steele was very surprised to see an open box of fireworks lying on the Fire Station path.

"Tut . . . tut . . . tut!" he snapped. "This is shocking! I'd better move these to a safe place before there's an accident." He picked up the box, carried it into his office and locked the fireworks away in his cupboard.

"Oh no!" groaned Norman. "Now there'll be trouble," and he set off back into town as fast as he could.

A few minutes later, Station Officer Steele came out and followed him down the hill towards Pontypandy.

They had just disappeared from view when Fireman Sam came striding out of the garage.

"What's going on?" he cried. "Where are my fireworks?"

He looked around but there was nobody about, nobody except Fireman Elvis Cridlington cooking dinner in the Fire Station kitchen.

"Elvis, have you seen a big box of fireworks?" asked Fireman Sam.

"I haven't seen anything but this pan of soup all day," moaned Elvis. "Why is it always so lumpy?"

"Never mind that!" said Fireman Sam. "This is much more important. Who on earth could have taken it?"

"Well, I did see that Norman hanging around earlier, and come to think of it, he was looking a bit guilty," said Elvis.

"Mmmm, yes, he *was* very interested in my boxes of fireworks," said Fireman Sam. "He said he wanted to set off all the fireworks himself."

"Well, there you are," said Elvis. "You'd better get down to Dilys's and see what he's up to, fast!"

Norman arrived home and slipped inside. There was nobody in the shop and he knew his mum was in the kitchen, because he could hear her singing at the top of her voice as she washed up the dishes.

"I think I'll pinch a bit of that bonfire toffee," thought Norman, spotting a jar on the counter. He picked out the biggest bit and shoved it into his mouth.

"Mmmmmm . . . that's nice," he mumbled.

He didn't realise it was everlasting toffee, the sort that fills up your mouth and goes on and on and on.

A moment later, Fireman Sam burst into the shop.

"NORMAN!" he called. "Where are my fireworks?"

Norman's eyes nearly popped out of his head.

"Gloogle-bloogle burble-wurble!" he went, trying to speak through his mouthful of toffee.

"Don't mess about with me, Norman. Did you take those fireworks?" asked Fireman Sam.

Dilys rushed in with wet, soapy hands.
"What's going on?" she cried.
"I think Norman's taken some of my fireworks," said Fireman Sam. "And I want to know where they are."
"NORMAN!" gasped Dilys. "How could you do such a naughty thing?"
"Gloogle-woogle burble-wurble!" choked Norman.
"Don't talk to me like that," snapped his mother. "Tell Fireman Sam where those fireworks are, this minute!"
"Oooh-aaah! Yah-boo!" dribbled Norman.

"Right! That's it!" cried Dilys. "If you won't tell Fireman Sam where you've hidden the fireworks, then you're not going to the party tonight."

"Blah-boooooooo!" spluttered Norman.

"Go to your room," ordered Dilys. "And stay there until I tell you to come down."

Norman was furious.

"Bloogle-burble, blah-bleh-nah!" he bawled.

"I won't listen to another word," said Dilys, and left poor Norman sulking in his bedroom.

Up at the Fire Station, Sarah and James were waiting for Fireman Sam.

"Can we watch you set up the fireworks?" asked Sarah.

"Yes, you can," answered Fireman Sam. "Though there won't be as many fireworks as I'd hoped. Norman's taken the second box of fireworks and I don't know where he's hidden it."

"Gosh!" said James. "I never thought Norman would be *that* naughty."

"Neither did I," said Fireman Sam. He sorted out the fireworks and took them over to the big platform he and Elvis had built earlier that day.

"Now listen carefully," he said. "You can stand close up now, but tonight, when I'm setting off the fireworks, you must stay right away from them, with everybody else."

"We will, Uncle Sam," promised the twins.

"You must never go near a lighted firework," said Fireman Sam. "And you must never, ever touch one, even if you think it's gone out. It may still be lit and it could suddenly go off in your face. Then you'd have to spend Bonfire Night in the hospital. You wouldn't like that."

"No, we wouldn't!" cried Sarah and James.

“Right then, let’s get started,” said Fireman Sam. “These are the Catherine wheels. I’ll nail them to the platform, nice and firm, so they can whizz round, but won’t fall off.

“And here are the rockets,” he added, taking them out of the box.

“Hey! Brilliant big rockets,” said Sarah.

“That’s right,” said Fireman Sam. “These will go in these tubes I’m sticking in the ground.”

“Why?” asked James.

"So that they will fly straight up into the sky," said Fireman Sam. "Now, we've got volcanoes, roman candles, cascades and snow fountains. These will all go on the platform, so everybody will have a good view. I'm going to put a rope across the path, right here and everybody must stand behind it, well back from the fireworks."

By the time they'd finished it was getting dark.

"Time to light up the night," laughed Fireman Sam. "Let's get the bonfire going."

When everybody in the town saw the fire crackling and blazing, they rushed up the hill to the Fire Station.

"Oh, how beautiful," sighed Bella.

"That's just the start," said Fireman Sam, and he lit the first rocket.

WHOOOOOOOOSH! It shot up into the dark sky, a flash of gold and a trail of dazzling pink stars.

"OOOOOH!" cried the crowd.

The roman candles were next. They exploded in a rush of blazing yellow, and then the volcanoes spurted out bright fountains of silver and gold.

"AAAAAH!" gasped the crowd.

The Catherine wheels whirled and swirled in a glittering shower of red and blue and green.

"WHEEEEEEE!" laughed the crowd, and then the last rocket whistled across the sky and it was all over.

"MORE! MORE!" shouted the crowd.

"Sorry, there aren't any more," said Fireman Sam.

"Oh yes there are!" said Station Officer Steele, and he stepped forward with a big box of fireworks.

"Here," he said. "Have these."

"What!" spluttered Fireman Sam. "But they're mine! I bought them this morning. Where did you find them?"

"They were lying on the path right outside my office," said Steele. "Very dangerous, I thought. So I locked them up, nice and safe in my cupboard."

"Oh no!" groaned Fireman Sam. "I've made a *terrible* mistake." He left Elvis and Station Officer Steele in charge of the bonfire and hurried down the hill to Pontypandy.

Down at Dilys's, Norman had been trying to watch the firework display from his bedroom window, but the tree outside blocked his view.

"Bother this!" he thought. "I'm going to sneak out and get a better look at those fireworks."

He wriggled through the window and started to climb down the tree. R-I-P! went his trousers, as they caught on a branch. No matter how he struggled, he couldn't get free.

Dilys was very surprised to see Fireman Sam standing on her back doorstep.

"Hello, there," she said. "What can I do for you?"

"I've come to take Norman to the party," said Fireman Sam. "He didn't take the fireworks. Station Officer Steele had them. I'm very sorry I accused Norman of doing such a bad thing."

"My poor boy!" cried Dilys. "I'll call him down at once."

But Norman wasn't in his room.

"Help! Help!" he yelled. "I'm out here, stuck in the tree!"

Fireman Sam couldn't climb up and Norman couldn't climb down.

"Hang on Norman!" called Fireman Sam. "I'll send for Jupiter."

Auxiliary Fireman Trevor Evans was on duty that night. He drove Jupiter down to Pontypandy and parked her beneath the tree, then extended the ladder as far as it would go. Fireman Sam climbed up.

"Please be careful!" shouted Dilys. "Don't drop him!"

Fireman Sam unhooked Norman's trousers and held him firmly over his shoulder.

"Steady now," he said, and climbed down to Dilys.

"Oh thank you, Fireman Sam," she cried. "Thank you for rescuing my boy."

"That's quite all right, Dilys," said Fireman Sam. "I think I owe Norman an apology."

"What!" gasped Norman. "Aren't you angry with me?"

"Certainly not," answered Fireman Sam. "I know now that it wasn't you who took those fireworks. It was Officer Steele. I'm very sorry I got things wrong Norman, and I'm even sorrier that you missed half of the party. But if we hurry we'll be in time to see the second lot of fireworks."

Trevor Evans drove Fireman Sam, Dilys and Norman up the hill to the Fire Station where everyone was waiting. Station Officer Steele and Elvis Cridlington had just finished setting up the second lot of fireworks. Fireman Sam lit the first rocket. It was a brilliant big one.

Norman jumped for joy.

"That's it!" he yelled. "That's the one I was looking for!"

WHOOOOOOOSH! The rocket raced across the sky, followed by another and another and another!

Finally, when all the fireworks were finished, everybody stood around the dying fire and shared out their supper. Bella had brought some parkin. Station Officer Steele had brought some lemonade. Sarah and James had brought some gingerbread people. Elvis had baked lots of potatoes and made some pasties. And Dilys had brought a large jar of bonfire toffee . . .

"Help yourself," said Dilys, and Norman passed the jar around with a secret smile on his face.

"Thanks," said Sarah and James.

"Nice," said Bella.

"Mmmm, I do like a bit of toffee," said Officer Steele.

Everyone had a great big piece of toffee except Norman.

"Bloogle-woogle!" spluttered Fireman Sam.
"Burble-wobble" giggled Bella.
"Na-blub-glub-glub!" gnashed Officer Steele.
"Haa-haa-yah-boo!" went the twins.
"Hee! Hee! Hee!" roared Norman. "Now you know why I was all stuck up. It's everlasting toffee and it goes on and on and ON!"

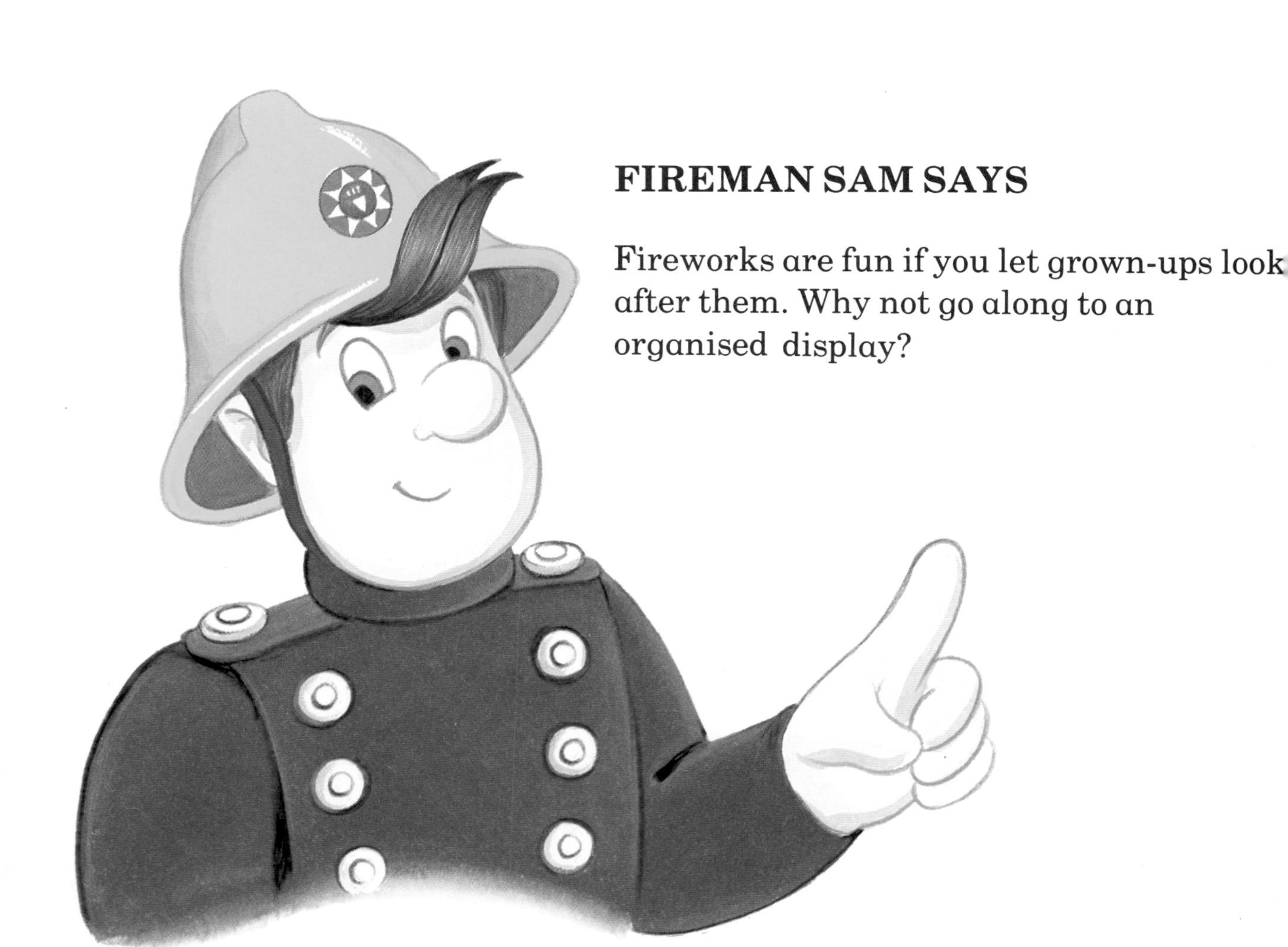

FIREMAN SAM SAYS

Fireworks are fun if you let grown-ups look after them. Why not go along to an organised display?

Fireman Sam and the Farm Fire

story by Caroline Hill-Trevor
illustrations by The County Studio

Developed from a storyline by Rob Lee
and a script by Nia Ceidiog

It was a very hot afternoon and Jupiter was returning to Pontypandy after the third fire that day.

"Well, I certainly hope that was the last fire for a while," said Fireman Sam. "It's too hot to be putting out fires – We'd be better off at the seaside."

"You're right, Sam," replied Station Officer Steele, wiping his face with a big red hanky. "But blazing hot weather like this means a lot of fires. Isn't that right Cridlington?"

"Sarah and James look as if they'd rather be at the seaside too," said Elvis as they pulled up beside Bella's potato patch.

"Hello there you two," said Fireman Sam. "Picking potatoes... Not exactly the weather for chips, is it? Maybe Bella's making some of her special potato salad," he said hopefully.

"No, Uncle Sam, it's for ice cream," answered Sarah, looking hot and bothered.

"Um," said Elvis looking puzzled, "I've never heard of potato ice cream – it must be new."

"Oh Elvis, Bella is going to give us some ice cream if we fill the buckets with potatoes for her – not make ice cream out of them!" said James impatiently. "Come on Sarah, the harder we work, the sooner we'll be finished."

"Rightio, we'd best be getting back as well. Keep up the good work Sarah!" said Fireman Sam, looking thoughtful.

When Jupiter had driven out of sight Sarah and James stopped for a break and noticed a wisp of smoke billowing from the hillock overlooking the potato patch.

"There can't be another fire," cried Sarah.

"It could be coming from a barbecue I s'pose," said James. "Come on – it's safest to check anyway."

They ran up the hill.

"Oh no! It's the barn at Pandy Lane Farm. What about the animals?" shouted James. "There's a call box down the road – we must get Jupiter out quickly."

Breathlessly Sarah dialled 999 and asked for the Fire Service.

Jupiter was back at the Fire Station. The crew had just sat down with a cup of tea when the alarm went off. Fireman Sam tore the details off the printer.

"Fire at the barn at Pandy Lane Farm," he read out. "Right, let's get going."

Fireman Sam, Station Officer Steele and Elvis slid down the pole and leapt into the cab without wasting a second.

For the fourth time that day Jupiter set out with the siren wailing.

"Mama Mia, another fire" said Bella, watching Jupiter rush through the village.

"Looks serious. Where's my Norman got to now?" said Dilys Price, looking around nervously. "He set out with a picnic and his fishing rod hours ago. I hope he's not in any trouble."

As the Firemen approached Pandy Lane Farm, they met Trevor driving his bus back towards Pontypandy.

"Turn around and follow us, Auxiliary Fireman Trevor Evans," commanded Station Officer Steele. "We're going to need all the help we can get. Speed up Cridlington, never mind the bumps," he ordered as they turned down the track leading to the farm.

PONTYPANDY
BWS 4937

Together Elvis and Fireman Sam manned the hose and the water gushed out – WHOOSH!

"Oh no," remembered Fireman Sam, "we didn't check the water level in Jupiter's tank. Let's hope we've got enough. We must stop this fire spreading."

"Come on Trevor – you've a way with animals, we must move them," said Station Officer Steele, as a frightened hen zoomed overhead squawking. "Get the cows and the donkey out, and don't forget the ducks."

“I hope this isn’t the stubborn kind of donkey,” muttered Trevor as he tied a rope round its neck. It wasn’t. The next moment Trevor found himself flying out of the barn in a flurry of feathers as the geese also made their escape, honking angrily.

Trevor chased out all the cows and ducks, but just as he and Station Officer Steele were congratulating themselves, Sarah and James pointed at the barn roof.

"Look up there Trevor – some hens are trapped in the rafters – they'll get burnt," shouted Sarah.

"Don't you worry Sarah, we'll save them," said Station Officer Steele. "We'll get the ladder out. Fireman Evans is going up."

Trevor quickly climbed the ladder and shooed the hens out, waving one arm and holding on tightly with the other hand. “Good with animals I may be,” he thought to himself, “but these hens are giving me vertigo.”

But just as all the animals were out of the barn and the fire was finally under control the hose started to splutter. Instead of whooshing out the water slowed to a trickle.

"What shall we do now?" said Elvis. "We still have to damp everything down. I know! Find a hydrant."

"No hydrants out here in the wilds, Elvis," pointed out Fireman Sam.

“Well, a drain’ll have to do then,” said Elvis, thinking quickly.

“Good thinking Cridlington,” said Station Officer Steele, looking relieved.

“Uh, Sir, there are no drains out here either,” said Fireman Sam, “but there is a pond down the road – let’s get down there double quick, before the fire flares up again.”

They jumped into Jupiter and drove off down the road to fill up the tank with pond water. When they left the pond was almost empty.

Norman Price had been fishing quietly by the pond all afternoon and had fallen asleep after his picnic.

“Oh no, now what’ve I done?” he said, waking up to see the pond emptying. “Beginner’s luck – I can’t catch a fish but I have caught the plug, and pulled it out, by the look of things. Better get out of here before anyone comes.” And he hurried off towards Pandy Lane Farm.

Back at the farm the crew damped down the fire with the pondwater.

"You were all terrific," said James.

"What a good job you remembered that pond, Uncle Sam," said Sarah. "It's lucky no fish live in it!"

"Shoo, shoo, shoo. Get out of my bus, you ungrateful birds. Fine thanks for rescuing you, this is, Ssss! Ssss!" said Trevor, running at the hens with both arms waving.

"Whatever's all that noise," said Fireman Sam, turning round to see. "Oh look, Trevor Evans and his amazing travelling chicken run. Poor Trevor!"

Norman came up. “What’s been going on? Have I missed the excitement?”

“Hello Norman, been fishing – did you catch anything?”

Norman went bright red. “Only the plug. I fell asleep and now the pond’s empty – I must’ve pulled it out.”

“Well I wouldn’t worry about it, if I were you, Norman,” said Fireman Sam, winking at Sarah and James. “We used the water to damp down this fire. Now let’s see about Bella’s potatoes. Can I borrow your fishing rod please Norman?” He led the way back to the pond.

Using Norman's fishing rod Fireman Sam pulled a bicycle and an old pram out of the pond and made them into a very strange contraption. Sarah looked puzzled.

"Brill, Uncle Sam, but ... what is it?"

"Let me demonstrate the Samuel Patent Potato Picker," Fireman Sam said proudly. He pushed it up the field and quickly filled the buckets.

"Thanks Uncle Sam, that's great," said Sarah and James together.

“O Bellissima, now I know who the best potato pickers are; thank you, thank you,” said Bella when she saw all the potatoes.

"Uncle Sam helped us," said Sarah.
"Yes, but you helped us too," said Station Officer Steele.
"Then you all deserve my best Italian ice cream."

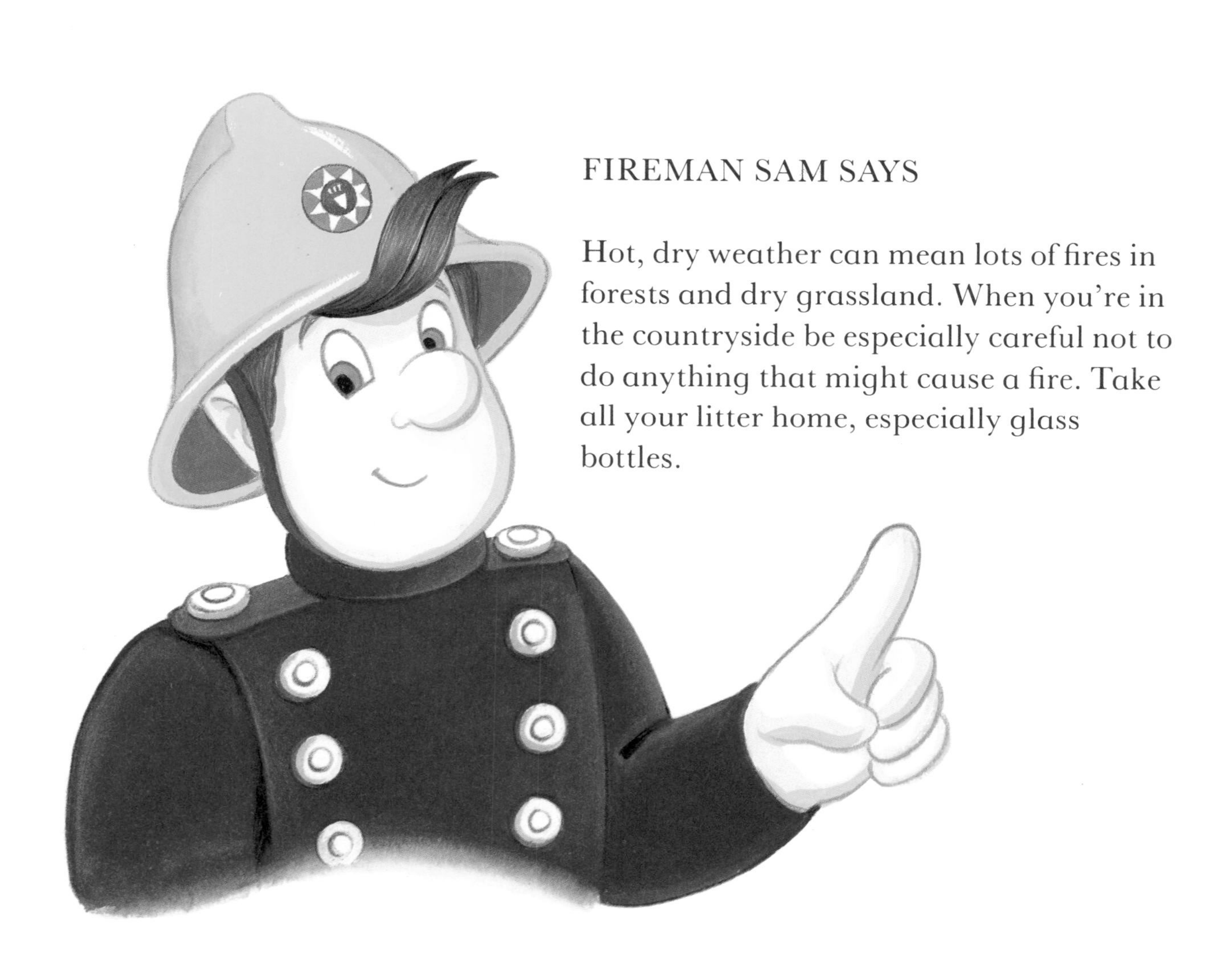

FIREMAN SAM SAYS

Hot, dry weather can mean lots of fires in forests and dry grassland. When you're in the countryside be especially careful not to do anything that might cause a fire. Take all your litter home, especially glass bottles.

Fireman Sam and the Underground Rescue

story by Rob Lee
illustrations by the County Studio

Sarah and James were in Bella's cafe watching Bella pack a picnic hamper for them all.

"Yum yum!" drooled James, watching Bella pack jam sandwiches, fruit and crisps.

"And last but not least," said Bella triumphantly, ". . . . a special chocolate cake – my favourite!"

When they saw Bella's treat, the twins couldn't wait.

Just then Bella's cat, Rosa, jumped up onto the table, almost knocking over a bottle of orangeade.

"Careful, Rosa!" cried Bella.

"Miaoow!" Rosa mewed as she rubbed against the hamper.

"I think she wants to come on the picnic, too, Bella," chuckled Sarah. Bella looked doubtful but the twins pleaded.

"Oh, alright," said Bella at last, wrapping up a small piece of fish for Rosa and shutting the hamper. "If we hurry we can catch Trevor's bus to Pandy Lane."

"I'll carry the hamper," said James.

"I thought you might," said Bella as they left the cafe.

In Dilys Price's shop, her son Norman was packing his rucksack with fish hooks and bait tins.

"And where do you think you're going?" asked Dilys.

"Fishing, Mam," replied Norman.

"And who's going to help me in the shop, I'd like to know?" asked Dilys.

"Aw, Mam," groaned Norman, taking a tin from his pocket. "Have a sweet, Mam," he offered.

"You're Mummy's little darlin', aren't you?" cooed Dilys. "Of course you can go fishing." She took a sweet and shrieked. "YUK! It's a worm!" She dropped the wriggling worm and Norman ran out of the shop laughing.

"NORMAN!" cried Dilys. But Norman was halfway to Pandy Lane.

At the fire station, Penny Morris, from the Newtown brigade, was delivering a new supply of oxygen masks.

"You have a receiver and microphone in your mask," Penny explained, "so I can talk to you through this handset."

"Let's have a try," said Fireman Sam as he and Elvis put on the masks.

"Are you receiving me?" Penny spoke into the handset.

"Loud and clear!" replied Fireman Sam.

"Are you receiving me?" Penny asked Elvis. Elvis didn't reply. "Can you hear me?" Penny shouted into the receiver. Elvis took off his mask.

"Not much use these, Penny," he said. "All I can hear is Michael Jackson!"

"You're supposed to take your stereo off first!" sighed Fireman Sam.

"Oh, oh yeah," muttered Elvis, blushing.

Bella and the children had found a nice spot for their picnic.

"Ah, it's so peaceful here," sighed Bella as she unpacked the hamper.

"Except for the wasps," said Sarah, chasing one away.

"I don't know whether to have a jam sandwich first or the chocolate cake," said James.

"Just eat them both together," laughed Bella as she put Rosa's piece of fish on a plate.

Nobody had noticed Norman in the next field.

Norman hadn't noticed the picnickers either.

"I bet this river is packed with fish," he said as he busily baited his line. "Mam *will* be pleased when she sees all the fish I'll be taking home for tea."

Norman got ready to cast his line.

"Norman Price smashes the record: largest trout of the year caught in Pontypandy Pond!" he dreamt as he flicked the rod over his shoulder.

The line flew over the hedge behind Norman, towards the picnic party. Rosa looked up crossly as her fish was swept away from under her nose.

"My, you must have been hungry, Rosa," laughed Sarah. "You've cleaned your plate already!"

As Norman cast his line forward he was slapped on the back of his head by Rosa's fish.

"Strange," he muttered, "I'm catching fish on dry land!"

Curious, Norman peered over the hedge.

“Oooh! Bella’s having a picnic,” whispered Norman.

“Perhaps I should try a spot of jam buttie fishing for a change!”

Bella looked up in amazement as a jam sandwich flew up into the air.

“What on earth . . . ?” she gulped.

“Great shot!” cried Norman, reeling in the sandwich. “Now for a slice of that chocolate cake!”

But the next time Norman was not so lucky. His rod hit a wasps’ nest and a horde of angry wasps streamed out.

“Oh, no!” he cried as the wasps made straight for him. He jumped up and ran off across the field yelling “HELP! HELP!”

Norman ran as fast as he could until, finally, the wasps gave up.

"Phew!" he puffed as he stumbled through the deep grass. "I think I'm safe now."

Suddenly the ground gave way beneath him and he fell into a deep pit.

"Whooah!" Norman cried as he plunged downwards and landed with a bump. "It's d-dark in here," he stuttered, his voice echoing. "I'll never be able to climb back out, the sides are much too steep."

"Let's go for a walk," said Bella after they'd eaten. "Perhaps we can find my disappearing sandwich."

"I'll race you!" shouted James and he dashed off leaving Sarah behind.

"You started before me!" Sarah yelled back. "Watch out, Rosa! I'll trip over," she called as Rosa ran under her feet.

Looking over the hedge, James said, "Look! There's a rucksack."

"And a fishing rod," said Sarah, pointing further along the bank. "It looks like Norman's."

"I wonder where he is," said Bella.

"Come on, let's try and find him," said James.

When they came to the long grass Rosa pricked her ears.
"Do you hear something, Rosa?" asked Bella.
"I do!" cried James. "Listen!"
When they all stood quietly they heard a faint cry.
"Help! Help!"
Rosa dashed off.
"Quick! It's coming from over there!" called James, running towards the hole.
"Help!" cried the voice again.
"It's Norman!" said Sarah.
They all peered into the dark hole.
"Don't go too near the edge," Bella warned.

“Are you alright, Norman?” Bella yelled down into the pit.
“I think so,” replied Norman faintly. “But it’s too steep for me to climb back out.”
“Don’t worry,” Bella shouted back. “We’ll get help. James, you’d better run to the phone box in Pandy Lane and call the fire brigade.” James ran off as fast as he could.
Bella called to Norman.
“Stay where you are, Norman. Help is on the way.”

At the fire station, Station Officer Steele ripped the message from the telex machine.

"What's up, Sir?" asked Fireman Sam.

"It's Norman Price," replied Station Officer Steele. "He's fallen into a pit near Pandy Lane!"

"It's probably that old disused mine shaft!" said Fireman Sam as they hurried towards Jupiter.

"Grab the oxygen masks, Cridlington," barked Station Officer Steele. "...At the double!"

"Yes, Sir!" replied Elvis, jumping to attention.

"I'll follow you, Sam!" shouted Penny Morris, leaping into the rescue tender.

The convoy sped through the streets of Pontypandy. Trevor Evans was just turning his bus into Pandy High Street when he heard the sirens. He braked sharply and pulled over to the side to let the engines go past.

"Blow me, they're in a hurry," he muttered, watching them speed off into the distance.

Meanwhile, down the pit, Norman was getting restless.
"Stay where you are," called Bella. "If you wander off you may get lost."
"I can hear Jupiter!" cried James.
Soon the two engines appeared over the hill.
"Don't worry," Sarah shouted to Norman, "Uncle Sam's on his way."
"He'll soon have you out safely," soothed Bella.
Meanwhile, unnoticed, Rosa had spotted a butterfly and darted off across the field after it.

The engines screeched to a halt near the pit and the crew piled out.

Fireman Sam lowered a gas detector into the hole and called down to Norman.

"Are you hurt, Norman?"

"I don't think so," Norman replied forlornly.

"There's no sign of gas down there, Sir," said Fireman Sam.

"You'd better take the masks just in case, Fireman Sam," replied Station Officer Steele.

"You'll need a spare one for Norman," said Penny.

Fireman Sam and Elvis checked their oxygen supply while Penny tested for radio contact.

"Are you receiving me?" she asked, speaking into the handset.

"Loud and clear!" replied Fireman Sam and Elvis as they lowered themselves down into the pit.

Norman was relieved when he saw Fireman Sam and Elvis coming down the mine shaft towards him.

"Don't worry," called Fireman Sam when he reached the bottom. "We'll soon have you out of here."

He shone his torch and could just make out Norman, crouching in a tunnel to one side of the pit.

"Watch your footing, Elvis. There are lots of loose rocks," Fireman Sam warned as he made his way towards Norman.

"Righto, Sam. Oh... Oops!" replied Elvis, tripping over a large stone.

"Are you alright, Elvis?" asked Fireman Sam.
"Nothing broken, thanks, Sam," sighed Elvis.
Just then they heard a slight rumble as one or two rocks fell from the roof at the mouth of the tunnel.
"Wh-what's that?" asked Elvis.
"You must have dislodged a beam," answered Fireman Sam as the rumble got louder.
Quickly Fireman Sam moved them all further up the tunnel to safety and seconds later the roof caved in, completely blocking the tunnel mouth.

“Great fires of London!” coughed Fireman Sam. “That was close!”

“We can’t get back to the hole,” said Elvis. “What do we do now?”

“Well, the first thing is for Norman to have one of these,” said Fireman Sam, handing Norman an oxygen mask. “It’s very dusty down here,” he added as he fitted the mask on Norman.

Outside, at the edge of the hole, Station Officer Steele and Penny were waiting anxiously to hear what was going on when Bella suddenly realised that Rosa was missing.

"Where's that cat of mine now?" she wondered.

"Don't worry, Bella," said Sarah. "She'll come back when it's time for her tea."

But Rosa had chased the butterfly through the fields and into the wood before finally giving up. Tired of that game, she looked for something else to play at and trotted off to investigate an interesting-looking hole, half hidden by the bushes.

Inside the tunnel Fireman Sam called up Station Officer Steele on the intercom.

"There's too much rubble for us to move, Sir. We'll have to try and find another way out. There should be another entrance."

Fireman Sam, Elvis and Norman inched their way along the tunnel.

"Look, Fireman Sam, the tunnel forks," said Elvis peering through the gloom.

"Which way do we go?" asked Norman. Then suddenly they heard a "miaoow!"

Fireman Sam shone his torch down one of the tunnels.

"Look! There's Rosa!" he cried. "She didn't come in with us – there must be another way out."

Rosa scampered back down the tunnel into the darkness.
"Quick!" said Fireman Sam. "Let's follow her." And the three of them hurried down the tunnel after Rosa.
"Now where's she gone?" Norman asked.
"Miaow!" called Rosa again.
"There she is," said Norman, catching sight of her eyes shining in the dark.

"There!" cried Elvis, watching Rosa squeeze between the boards across the exit. "Rosa's saved us!"

But when they arrived at the boarded-up entrance Fireman Sam looked disappointed.

"Not so fast, Elvis," he said. "We'll never get through that gap and these boards are nailed up solid."

Meanwhile Rosa had scampered off across the fields.

Station Officer Steele was just about to contact the firemen on the radio when he heard a "miaow" behind him.

"My Rosa's come back," cried Bella, running forward to pick up her cat. But Rosa dashed off again before Bella could catch her.

"I think she wants us to follow her!" said Bella excitedly.

"Perhaps she knows where Uncle Sam is," said Sarah.

"Right!" ordered Station Officer Steele, taking command. "Follow that cat!"

Rosa ran across the fields with Bella, Sarah and James hot on her heels. Penny and Station Officer Steele followed in the two engines, racing over the bumpy ground.

"I hope Rosa's not taking us butterfly chasing," puffed Bella.

"Or wild goose chasing!" added Sarah.

"No," cried James, "I think Rosa's found the entrance to the mine."

The engines screeched to a halt at the entrance and Station Officer Steele jumped down.

"Anyone hurt?" he enquired briskly, peering through the gap in the boards.

"No, Sir. We're right as rain," replied Sam. "Or at least we will be when we get out of here."

"I'll have you out in no time," smiled Penny as she took a chainsaw from the locker of her rescue tender. "This should do the trick."

Penny pulled the cord and the saw roared into life.

"Stand well back," she called.

Inside, Fireman Sam, Elvis and Norman covered their ears as Penny quickly sawed through the wood. Sawdust flew everywhere and in no time the entrance was clear.

"Very efficient, I must say, Penny," said Fireman Sam admiringly as they all stepped out into the sunlight.

Everybody piled into the vehicles and they drove off towards Pontypandy.

"You've been very brave, Norman," said Station Officer Steele, "so just this once we'll use the sirens."

Norman beamed with excitement. "I should fall down mine shafts more often," he thought to himself.

The sirens were still blaring when they pulled up outside his mum's shop.

"Am I on fire?" asked Dilys, running outside.

Fireman Sam laughed and explained what had happened.

"But don't worry, Dilys," he soothed. "There's no harm done."

"Mummy's brave little boy," cooed Dilys, smothering Norman with hugs and kisses.

"Aw, Mam!"

Later that day, Fireman Sam and the crew were relaxing at Bella's when Norman appeared at the door carrying a plate of fish wrapped in a big bow.

"This is for Rosa, for fishing us out of the mine!" said Norman shyly.

"I'll second that," cheered Fireman Sam. "Congratulations, Firefighter Rosa!"

FIREMAN SAM SAYS:

Football is a good game but only play in wide open spaces where you won't break anything if you miss the ball.

This edition first published in Great Britain 1993
by Dean, an imprint of Reed Children's Books
Michelin House, 81 Fulham Road, London SW3 6RB
and Auckland, Melbourne, Singapore and Toronto
Reprinted 1993 (twice)

Based on the animation series produced by Bumper Films for
S4C/Channel 4 Wales and Prism Art & Design Ltd.
Original idea by Dave Gingell and Dave Jones assisted by
Mike Young. Characters created by Rob Lee.
Stories by Rob Lee, Diane Wilmer and Caroline Hill-Trevor.
Illustrations by The County Studio.

ISBN 0 603 55252 8

Produced by Mandarin Offset
Printed in Hong Kong